W9-BMF-562

# That Dancin' Dolly

A RETELLING OF "Buffalo Gals," a Traditional American Song

by Jennifer J. Merz

DUTTON CHILDREN'S BOOKS • New York

## A NOTE ABOUT THE SONG ON WHICH THIS BOOK WAS BASED

"Buffalo Gals" is a pre–Civil War minstrel song, originally titled "Lubly Fan." It was written by John Hodges, alias Cool White, circa 1844. He sang it around the country, inserting the name of the location where he was performing at the time before the word "Gals" (e.g., "Pittsburgh Gals," "Charlestown Gals," etc.). He performed it in Buffalo in 1848, and for some reason,"Buffalo Gals" stuck as the name of the song. Reportedly, it was a very popular dance tune in the 1800s.

This song was referred to in Mark Twain's *Tom Sawyer,* played at dances in Laura Ingalls Wilder's *Little House* books, and sung by Jimmy Stewart and Donna Reed in the movie *It's a Wonderful Life.* In the 1940s, it was made into a dance hit called "Dance With a Dolly (With a Hole in Her Stockin')."

## ABOUT THE ART

The pictures in this book are handcrafted collages, with all design elements cut or torn from various special papers, laces, and trimmings, and details painted in gouache.



CIP Data is available.

Published in the United States by Dutton Children's Books,
a division of Penguin Young Readers Group
345 Hudson Street, New York, New York 10014
www.penguin.com
Designed by Irene Vandervoort
Manufactured in China First Edition

ISBN 0-525-47214-2

1 2 3 4 5 6 7 8 9 10

To Ken, Lesley, and my special coach, Julia;

and especially

To Pat, for the dolly and so much more, with love always

As I was
going out to play,

Sing and play,
Sunny day,

My special doll said, "Come, let's play!"
And I said, "I love you!"

I asked her if she'd like to dance,

Sing and dance,

run and prance.

My favorite doll would like to dance!

Let's dance through the whole afternoon.

Oh, I

Danced!

with my dolly with the hole in her stockin',

And my knees kept a-knockin'.

And my toes kept a-rockin'!

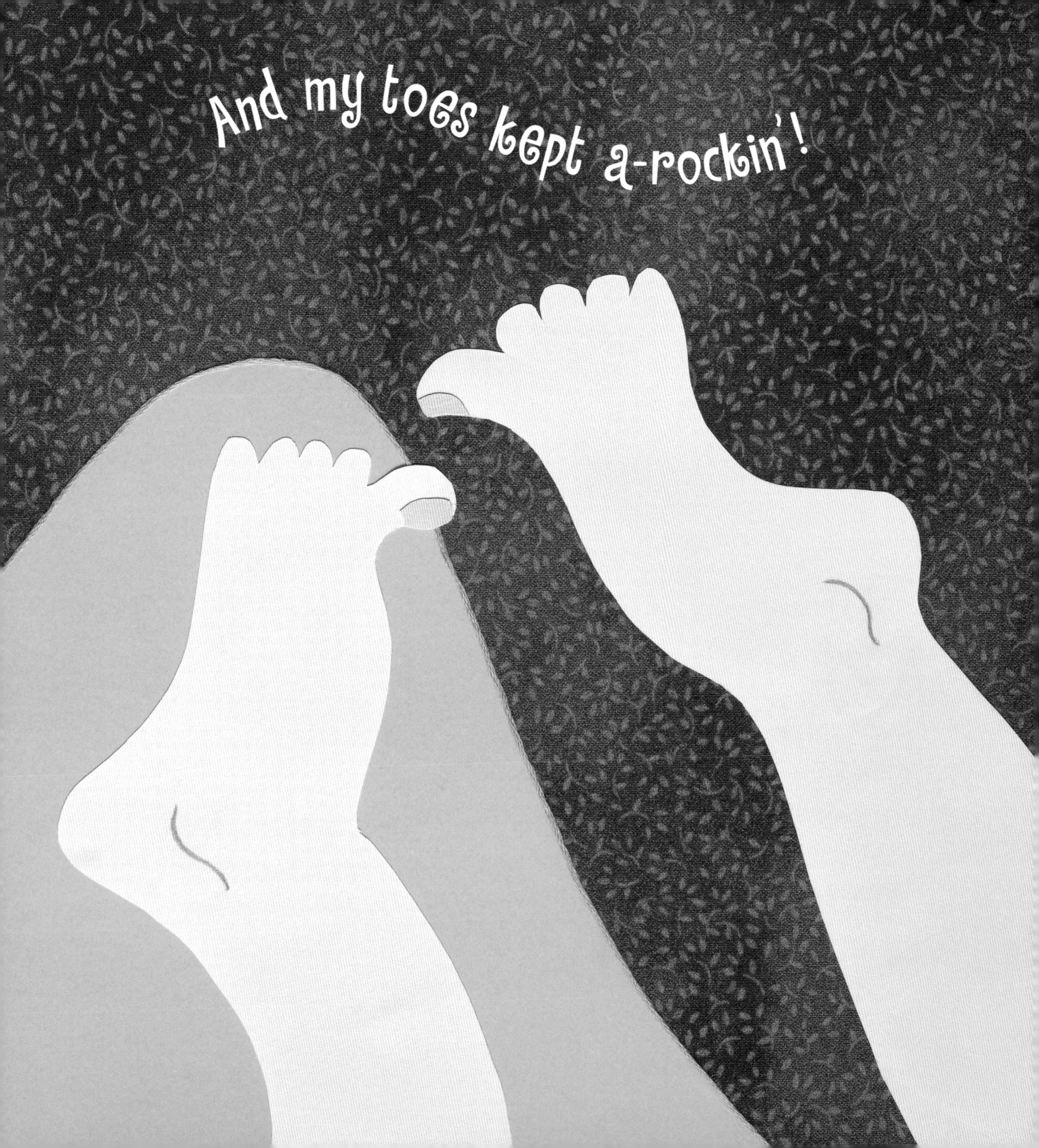

Danced!

with my dolly with the hole in her stockin',

And we danced by the light of the moon.

# That Dancin' Dolly

A RETELLING OF "BUFFALO GALS,"
A TRADITIONAL AMERICAN SONG

As I was go - ing out to play, sing and play, sun - ny day, my
spe - cial doll said, "Come, let's play!" And I said, "I love you!" I
asked her if she'd like to dance, sing and dance, run and prance. My
fav - 'rite doll would like to dance! Let's dance through the whole af - ter - noon. Oh, I
danced! with my dol - ly with the hole in her stock - in', and my knees kept a - knock - in', and my
toes kept a - rock - in'! Danced! with my dol - ly with the hole in her stock - in', and we
danced by the light of the moon.